BIGFOOT
and
Bunyip

BY NED EVETT

Illustrations by SMI Media

Special thanks: Rai Thistlewayte, Atlanta Hotel Bangkok, Stuart Tanner, Amine Kouider

In loving memory: Hope and Stuart Evett, George Paul Simitzes

CONTENTS

I , a wise and moderately ancient fool of Redding, Connecticut, and being of sound mind and not entirely bankrupt of heart, do hereby commit this secretive journal into the hands of whoever has chanced upon it in the fullness of time.

Bravo indeed! As you have now discovered, I chose the hollow base in my garden statue of Pan as the hiding spot for this modest volume. Perhaps it is scarcely worth a glance, save for one salient point: it contains the stark, unvarnished truth regarding my comrades Bigfoot, Bunyip, and an assortment of extraordinary beings who fall outside the narrow confines of our vaunted species.

We humans are all too smug in our dominion over the lesser brethren of this verdant world, so my thanks to you for finding and reading this nuntius occultis, although I must admit it may not be of the quality of my public (and much beloved) work, achieved during the hot blooded decades of my youth and long, fruitful days of middle age blessed by fame and financial independence. Also be aware dear reader that this is not the sole volume of these fantastic tales, and if by the end of reading you wish more, then more you must seek!

Weariness has, over time, taken its toll on me—the loss of children, cherished friends, my beloved wife, compounded by the assorted atrocities of these modern times, war, plague, ad infinitum. My sight dims, my ears sometimes catch sounds, more often they do not, and the once cherished taste of tobacco has turned as bitter and as desiccated as a spent leaf. The few pleasures that remain flicker in the distance like the last embers of a once roaring fire. And oh, what splendid blazes they were, mind you, dear reader.

Now, as you hold this secret yankee cipher, this voice echoing through who knows how many decades, allow me to recount tales of valor and intrigue. Let me narrate the grand brawls in Melbourne's Arena, of characters named Disraeli, Churchill, and the eccentric Phosphorous Dan. Herein are tales of those who hunt and those hunted, of the struggle for freedom—a saga of the extraordinary, penned by yours truly, Samuel Clemons, aka Mark Twain.

CACOPHONIES IN THE NIGHT

In the summer of 1893 I was invited by the good citizens of Melbourne to hold forth in lecture at their new Opera house in New South Wales, Australia. The letter of invite arrived via courier from San Francisco, where I had famously nearly frozen to death ten summers previously.

I was already composing my refusal of the invitation due the enormous distances involved, but had yet to see the suggested fee (plus expenses!) at the conclusion of their most sincere request. In other words, they set forth a figure that spoke louder and with greater eloquence than any phrase I could muster in declination.

Why such a lofty fee? The answer is as plain as gold! Australia is gold country, gold of such quantity as to make purveyors of culture in her cities lose all perspective when securing cultural emissaries to speak within her borders. Namely, aptly, yours truly, no stranger to steamer trunks and state dinners aboard tea clippers and the new ironclads. These speaking engagements afford me the great luxury of time to write, to smoke, and to think. Indeed, the advent of steam power and the great canal of Suez has cut transit time by a neat third, requiring me to bring less tobacco, even less whiskey, and a somewhat lessened parcel of pen and parchment.

Upon accepting the offer to speak in Melbourne I decided to visit for the first time the forests of the Puget Sound in the newly chartered state of Washington. I was to inhabit a perfectly lonely cabin in the deep woods before embarking for Melbourne aboard the HMS Erasmus from the tiny port city of Seattle. I arrived in Seattle via transcontinental rail from Chicago in mid September, 1893, and was taken to the cabin by the owner himself, a Chinese named Yuan Tsu, whose flavored English was a fine match to my starched Yankee American. He had 'purchased' the land and cabin in a poker game five years previously, and explained to me on our two days' journey by wagon that as much frontier commerce resolved on the inside straight as it did the contract and humble ledger.

Upon arrival I bid Yuan Tsu adieu, and robustly set about finishing a whole host of writings delayed for months by the constant stream of literary pilgrims, tax collectors, and well wishers to my Connecticut home. I spent my days there happily in that cabin, a small stream next to my bedroom window, my pipe, pen, and ten pounds of hard tack and beans. A month had gone by in this shrine of pine and pitch when, late one rainy night, I heard the strangest sound of all my days.. It was a cry of anguish, human, but decidedly not so, as if twenty men of the lowest bass baritone had cried out in perfect horror and in unison. The soft pop of gunfire along with the howls of dogs arrived to my much younger ears in due course, the calamity muted by the dense woods and distance. After some fifteen minutes the distant cacophony subsided. I doused the whale-oil lamp by my bedside and slept ill that night for the echo of it all.

Yuan Tsu appeared at my doorstep as dawn broke the following day, ready to whisk me off for Seattle, the HMS Erasmus, and Melbourne. With the morning light barely touching the tips of the mighty trees, I couldn't help but inquire if the local wildlife—perhaps a mountain lion or bear—were known to vocalize in such a manner that could curdle the blood, or if perchance some rugged trapper or mountain man had come to a grim demise in these parts. Upon hearing my question, Yuan's face took on a solemn, bitter cast, as if the shadows of every sorrowful tale in the woods had suddenly decided to settle upon his features.

"No man, no bear." he said. "We go." I packed my few belongings and we rode in silence aboard his wagon down the narrow road through the woods. His horses, two brownish paints, were a bit slight in the gait for working a buckboard, and seemed uneasy at something as we made our way.

Later that morning, about fifteen miles from my logged retreat, we happened upon fifteen men in city clothing limping down the road. Several of them carried odd looking rifles, scanning the woods and barely taking note of our passing. The rifles were breech-loaded with clear glass barreling in which tiny feather-vaned darts sat chambered. As we approached my cordial 'good morning' was met with an ill, chilled silence. Upon perambulating closer I noticed several of the men sporting fresh contusions, smatterings of blood, and gingerly cradling unset broken arms and shoulders. I lit my pipe to calm my nerves. Between puffs of smoke I could see more of their party one hundred feet off the main road in the woods, shovels in hand, a pile of dead hounds laying next to a massive amount of hemp rope. Scores of trees as big as ten men had been broken in half as if pulled to earth by an Elephant of deepest Africa.

"We go now." hissed Yuan, our welfare at the hands of these strange men certainly upon his mind.

Around the next bend in the road we happened upon deep ruts carved in the mud nearly twice the width of the narrow road through the woods. Saplings and ferns along the side of the path had been shunted aside like the waves from a paddle wheel on the mighty Mississip'. A great thumping sound filled the mountains as we drew closer to some great unseen force on the road in front of us. Yuan's look of unease deepened into a look of wanton self-preservation which I heartily shared.

"There is a high road that forks south, delaying us another day to port, but you'll make it." said Yuan. I nodded in perfect, silent agreement.

We wove in and out of huge muddy ruts for a mile until finding the fork towards Olympia, guiding the skittish horse and the buckboard over a stony rise. Three miles later with the great rumbling sound moving away, Yuan Tsu brought the whineying team to a halt, quieting them softly in Chinese. Through a stand of Olympic Pine we saw a strange contraption, iron-clad and coal black, born upon four brass and steel cog-shaped wheels. It belched smoke and looked massive to our straining eyes nearly two miles down the mountain on the main road. More men with rifles flanked the lumbering beast as it trundled towards Seattle.

"Forget this day in your books, Mark Twain." said Yuan Tsu "These men will bring death if you write of it."

"Yes." I said, slowly puffing my pipe. "Yes I believe they would."

Yuan Tsu relentlessly drove the horses through the night and arrived at the Port of Seattle the next evening, well in time for my embarkation aboard the HMS Erasmus. One of his horses had become lame from the achievement, and the last I saw of Yuan Tsue he was carefully loading his black powder revolver in front of the Pike Street Butcher, preparing to recoup one final investment from the animal. They began to bargain as I slipped towards the docks.

The HMS Eramus lay gleaming at its berth as indicated, an ironclad marvel of this new age, of the annihilation of time and distance shared with its landward brethren the steam locomotive. My steamer trunk and sundry possessions for the journey had been delivered according to the steward as I presented credentials and documents of passage. As I placed the documents back in my valise, a short, nasty, warthog of man collided with my left hip on his hasty way up the gangplank. In 1874 my hip had been broken in a bar room brawl in Silver City, Nevada, following a confrontation with the local mine boss unhappy with my daily column in his weekly gazette. The warthog's black curly hair tumbled about his brow as I cried out in alarm and some amount of pain.

"I'm terribly sorry, Mr.?" the cad asked, clearly not recognizing me, which was no small injury to my bruised ego, to say nothing of my bruised hip. He took a step down the gangplank.

"Twain." I said, giving the fool one last chance to realize the stature of the national treasure he had just wounded. I jest dear reader, but only half so. His gin blossom and rosebush face lit up like a Carnaby Street Christmas tree at the sounding of my name.

"Oh, MARK Twain?" he softly gushed in the cold night air, gripping my hand with an earnest handshake politicians and gamblers have all perfected. Warm, but keenly seeking insights into the mind behind the hand gripped.

"When I read your name upon the manifest I nearly sought out a bigger vessel for our journey." he chirped.

"You flatter me quite well, Sir." I said. "The Erasmus is under your charter?"

"Yes she is, a fine ship, only out of Portsmouth this August, her boilers itching for the deep Pacific. Jennings, see that Mr. Twain's belongings are taken to the master guest suite; he is to have a key to the spirits cabinet of course. You drink Whiskey, yes Mr. Twain?" he said, his face narrowing like a fox.

"Indeed I do, Kentucky label mostly, we Americans are a corn mashing rabble as you've probably heard." I said, my Yankee distrust of his free Whiskey kicking in. The nectar within a pitcher planet is free to any insect wishing to drink, free room and board for eternity as well!

"May I also get your name, in addition to this bourbon-ous bounty?" I asked.

"Oh of course, I'm *Lord* Disraeli, Earl of Beaconsfield, KG, PC, former servant of Her Majesty Queen Victoria's kingdom but now deliciously retired from her service, for the most part. Forgive me for only having the best Whiskey in the world aboard the Erasmus and not your beloved.. Kentucky.. sour mash." his face puckered in disgust as if drinking some Blue Mountain hootch directly from a rusty still pipe.

"No worries Mr. Disraeli, that will do just fine." I said, gingerly inching my way up the gangplank with my singing hip.

"LORD Disraeli, Mr. Twain, oh and terribly sorry about the hip old boy. I myself have several war wounds from my time in Parliament." said Disraeli, shadowing me up the gangplank into the main receiving gangway.

"Well, Lord Disraeli, I'm bushed from a rather eventful journey here to embark for Melbourne, and I bid you a good night." I said, as a shot rang out from Yuan Tsu's revolver, some blocks away.

THE H.M.S. ERASMUS

Lord Disraeli's man Jennings led me to the guest deck with my bags in tow, nimbly navigating the corridor like a man reared at sea. I stopped as we passed room 112, the number of my room indicated on my transit papers from the good folks in Melbourne.

"Mr. Jennings, you old sea fox, my room is here." I said, showing him the papers.

"Just Jennings, Sir." he said, looking at the document in the flickering whale-oil lamp light. He removed the ship's master key and opened the door. Inside lay a small, humble room with a writing desk not much bigger than the one at the cabin, with a small dresser drawer, wash basin, and whiskey nowhere to be seen.

"Ah yes, these are the accommodations paid for by the good citizens and former wanton criminals of Melbourne." he said as he shut the door. "Right this way sir, never mind those papers, Lord Disraeli has something more comfortable for you in mind."

Jennings took me around the corner where an elevator stood closed, its great brass frame gleaming dully in the dimly lit corridor. Jennings placed his master key in the lock opening the two glass doors. He quickly loaded in my belongings and soon we were heading to the upper decks. I could smell the burning coal from the engine room below the waterline wafting up into the elevator shaft. The doors crisply opened eight decks later onto a fantastic, electric lit promenade,

"This floor is only accessible to you, Mr. Disraeli, myself, and the Captain. Here is your own master key." Jennings said, placing a large skeleton key in my hand. "And here is your room sir."

Jennings opened a door of royal oak nearly seven inches thick, and within lay dare I say not a room, but a veritable palace at sea. New electric tungsten lamps illuminated every facet of the glorious marble and teak vaulted interior space, some fifty feet in width and twenty five in depth. Colorful carpets impossibly deep from lands unknown lay beneath furniture of the highest artisanship. There did not appear to be a bed nor wash basin, presenting a potential fly in the ointment of paradise.

"Not bad." I said, with as much understatement as could be mustered. "Where might a tired Yankee rest his head?"

Without saying a word Jennings pulled a thick velvet rope hanging near the green fainting couch. The left hand third of the room turned upon some mighty electric motor as a grand platform bed piled high with down comforters rolled into view. Beyond the bed lay a white porcelain clawfoot tub and mirrored wash-basin. A smoking jacket and black silk pajamas embroidered with "HMS Erasmus" lay neatly on the bed. I was truly, and utterly without words at the scale of the opulence before me, but two syllables managed to fight their way to my palette.

"Whiskey?"

THE CREATURE

I bid Jennings good night and spent the evening with a hot bath and flask of single malt whiskey so divine it made me yearn for subjugation by the kingdom that distilled it upon me. I changed into the black pajamas and fell asleep, dreaming of the cabin in the woods of the Puget Sound.

In my dream I was writing at my humble cabin desk by lamp-light, struggling to complete the merest turn of phrase. Harder and harder I tried until a storm began to thunder and shout outside the dwelling. The door blew open and a torrent of rain rushed inside, inundating my desk and obliterating the pages I'd slaved over so many weeks. A dark figure emerged in the doorway, illuminated by the flashes of lightning outside. From this creature of the night came the same cry of anguish I'd heard before in the woods, and I woke with a fright in my cabin aboard the Erasmus. I woke, the dream stopped, yet the anguished cry did not. On and on it went, accompanied by the grinding harmony of some great crane or winch, hoisting the cry ever closer until it reverberated as if within the bounds of the Erasmus itself.

My fear quickly gave way to my Yankee curiosity as I hastily pulled my boots over the silk pajama leggings. I grabbed the key to the elevator and opened my door to find Jennings standing there in the dark. He placed his hand firmly on my chest and with the other arm placed his index finger to his mouth as if to silence the disturbing symphony outside. The cries of turmoil continued until there came five loud pops, then finally an ill but welcome silence.

"What on earth is going outside?" I asked.

"I'm sorry Mr. Twain, nothing out of the ordinary I assure you. The Eramus often carries strange cargo from the new world to the old. Mr. Disraeli asks if you'd care to join him for lunch tomorrow after we embark." said Jennings, stifling a yawn given the late hour.

"We're not as new as we once were." I said, half awake at best, eager for an explanation but even more eager for sleep.

"Lord Disraeli will explain the situation tomorrow Mr. Twain, I think he means to anyway. So, begging your pardon sir, for your own safety, go back to bed." said Jennings.

"You have a deal young Jennings, but I'll have my full say and sense about me tomorrow at lunch, so please inform Lord Disraeli to be ready."

And with that I concluded my first day and night aboard the HMS Erasmus. Around dawn the Erasmus pulled out of port, her great horn echoing through the streets of Seattle, recently rebuilt following a terrible fire. The blasts of the horn rattled me from a short yet sound sleep which had recovered the best of my faculty for creative application. I pulled my writing board from my steamer trunk along with some fine Missouri Pipe Tobacco, and set about writing the first few lines of the story you read now. In time they would be joined by the words of beasts, and other players in this tale, their accounts relayed to me by various means and methods, then duely transcribed to the best of my abilities. First amognst these accounts was the creature Bigfoot.

I, BIGFOOT

My life began in a cave, cool, deep, hidden. The bodies of my kind age slowly, one year for every twenty in the life of a man, and for nearly all of these years men had been pushing us deeper into hiding. My great-grandfather had seen the first men in canoes arrive from the north as the ice vanished. By the time I was born the white men from the east had arrived with different ways, possessing the same fear of the great unknowns present in these lands. I alone amongst my kind have learned the ways of men and this is how I am able to write these things to you. Their ways were made plain to me early on.

First, they killed my mother. Ambushed one morning whilst picking roots, I felt her tight grip on me as she ran away from the Suquamish men with their arrows. Looking up I remember her face with the morning sun above, her cold breath pushing in and out as we ran. So close we came to escaping like many other times before it. But the hunter this morning was very lucky in his aim, and when she fell I flew from her arms down the side of the ravine where we picked blackberries in the fall. My thick hair sliced through the brambles, hiding me from sight but not smell, and soon the men closed in on my hiding place.

As they struggled down the ravine, a white man burst through the brambles. I froze, still too young to fight, still a baby. I closed my eyes and waited. The man bade me be quiet then placed me in a canvas bag and tied the top shut. From inside the bag I heard the explosions of his gun as he fired upon the Suquamish men. I could hear the whoosh of arrows as they fell all around us, until the men gave up. The white man backed down the ravine and soon I was bouncing around the back of his horse, tied to the horn of its saddle. I slept.

I awoke that night at his camp, he was a trapper named Charbonneau. He and his wife Sacagawea raised me as one of their own, their two of their children had died of scarlet fever. Ten years had passed, and I had learned to speak French, Shoshone, and some English. I had also grown some six feet. They made a massive buffalo robe for me which hid my body hair. When asked by the local trappers about my hairy face, Charbonneau just laughed and said my mother was a bear. Sacagawea groomed me with ivory handled scissors and a straight razor to make me look as human as possible. But soon I had grown to ten feet, and with sadness they allowed me to return home after fifteen of their years. Charbonneau had been hired to bring a new expedition of whites from the east to these lands, and he promised to return one day to hunt with me. I never saw them again.

I hunted and lived as my ancestors had for almost eighty years, but I had developed a taste for two of man's pleasures, tobacco and coffee. This meant trading with the fur trappers and some of their Indian counterparts, and for that I needed something to trade. As the game slowly began to disappear from too many people taking their meat and hides, I found something more valuable to them, gold. Inside the cave where my family lived for many years there was a seam of gold far below the surface. It took me two days of careful climbing to reach it, and each time I scraped enough off to keep me in leaf and bean for another few months. This ultimately led to my discovery and capture by the fiend Disraeli and his cohort.

Not wanting to squeeze my huge frame into the bowels of the cave every week, and because of a growing appetite for the bean Arabica during the cold winter months, I set upon bringing up a larger quantity of gold than usual. Greed undid me. Using Charbonneau's shovel, I was able to dislodge a huge amount of pure gold and return it to the surface. This took several days.

When I was finished I realized that I had missed my usual rendezvous with the trapper Charles Duncan Wallace, whose company I did not dislike. It was from him I learned a fair amount of English. Spoken mind you, writing was at that point of my life a senseless jumble of shapes over which I had no control nor comprehension. For that skill it took Twain. How he and I met I will now inform you.

Without Charles Duncan Wallace to trade with, I instead revealed myself to the Chinaman Yuan Tsu, a modest landowner of a small spread obtained in a game of chance. Yuan Tsu knew well of my existence, as I had saved him from a band of Suquamish ten winters ago. It was to his great astonishment that a creature of my size (nearly fifteen feet tall by then) could hold forth in conversation, even though my Mandarin was quite limited. Fortunately, trade speak is limited, how much do you want, how much will pay, etc, and we quickly came to accord. The problem became not the terms of our trade, nor the gold used to procure my vices, but my mere existence for those who would become my enslavers.

Yuan Tsu made the honest mistake of revealing my earthly existence to a Mr. Jennings, an agent of sorts for Lord Benjamin Disraeli of the nation of Great Britain. Indeed I knew of Great Britain through their Hudson Bay Company, with whom I had traded many furs through Charbonneau. Yuan Tsu traded a fantastic tale of a giant, talking monkey-man one night at a tavern in Seattle with Mr. Jennings, who unbeknownst to Yuan Tsu, was in the area looking for just a beast. Yuan Tsu kept the terms of our agreement and location of the deal secret, but in his drunken repair from the tavern that evening was followed by two of Jenning's associates.

A week later Yuan Tsu had his gold, and I had enough coffee and tobacco to remain outside the lure of men for several years. Yuan Tsu felt the trade wasn't fair and offered me firearms and alcohol in addition to the other sundries, but I refused him and bid him farewell. I planned on remaining in the cave for a few days before heading to the Walla Walla country some ways to the east. But before that I wanted to ride my whale, one last time. The ride itself was exhilarating, however I also needed something else, Salmon to dry for my journey.

YIP YIP!

A whale is best called using a spirited "YIP YIP!", my yip yip can be heard for ten miles up and down the coast and far out to sea. Whale riding for my kind goes back to when whales traded dry land for the ocean, untold generations before. A legend speaks of two of my kind who were friends. One of the friends stole the seasons food stores of the other. Winter arrived and the friend died from hunger, leaving his small children fatherless. In the spring his act of thievery was discovered by the tribe and he was forced to forever give safe passage to the orphaned children upon his back. Over time the children grew, making the burden of their transport painful. He fled to the ocean's shore to avoid this obligation, but the gods instead gave him a tail and blowhole, and banished him to the ocean for the rest of eternity. The rides of my kind upon his back would also continue for eternity. My father taught me to whale-ride, as his father had taught him, and his father, etc.

My whale and I had met when we were both young, darting in and out of the waves near our fall feeding grounds. My father taught me how to scoop salmon up by the fistful below the surface and toss them end over end to shore. This practice was an important source of protein for my kind, and key to our great height and size. I called my whale the morning of my capture and spent several hours near shore fishing and riding the huge waves coming from beyond the horizon. In exchange for this, we riders would pick sea lice and barnacles from the backs of our rides, and thus the tradition continued. I had noticed fewer and fewer whales returning each year, and feared for them their valuable oil that powered the lamps of the cities of men.

Upon returning to my cave I noticed the smell of men, however because of the great stinking quantity of fish in my arms I did not smell them quite soon enough. I later learned they had followed Yuan Tsu, then slowly built up a base camp some miles from me. A solitary man was also in the area at Yuan Tsu's cabin, who would've been killed had he discovered their camp. This man turned out to be Mark Twain.

I heard the low murmuring of voices as I entered the cave and dropped my armload of fish. Out of the woods came forty men and as many hounds, yelling and waving torches at me. I laughed at their torch gambit as fire was well known to me, each day brewing my beans in a kettle on a carefully tendered fire. Trapped against the face of the mountain that held the cave, I quickly realized these men were intent on capturing me, not killing me. Still, the situation was not good, and running would do no good, so I stood to fight. From every direction came huge hemp nets which I easily tore apart. I bore my teeth and yelled hoping to scare some of them off. Before I knew it the hounds had arrived and began tearing at the flesh of my legs, their handlers yelling to no avail in an attempt to reduce their savagery upon me. I began tossing the animals one by one forcefully into the cave, dashing them against the rocks. I felt great anger towards the men directing their bites upon me, and great pity for them but killed them nonetheless.

I was doing pretty well considering the odds and was thinking about climbing up the mountain and raining rocks down upon them all when I was struck with a dozen small darts fired from as many rifles. These were not the flintlocks favored by Charbonneau and offered to me by Yuan Tsu, but some other manner of firearm. I did not die, but felt a warm torpor creeping over my limbs. I became enraged, breaking off limbs from the trees at the mouth of the cave and hurtling them at the men. This did great damage to the lot of them. My legs, as thick as the tree trunks I'd been using as missiles, began to buckle from the poison in the darts. A man came forth with a great leather harness as I fell to my knees. As he placed the harness upon my head I tore him in half for good measure. Another took his place, and another, until finally with my sight dimming the harness locked shut. I let out one final cry of anger, of anguish, that was heard that night by one the one man innocent in this sordid slaving business, Mark Twain.

THE GREAT IRON HOLD OF THE ERASMUS

A t breakfast I had scarcely little appetite considering the turmoil of the events occurring the previous day. I dined alone with some coffee and a half eaten apple tart, making a list of questions for Lord Disaeli at lunch later that day. Nothing but ocean and blue sky was visible through the magnificent viewing portal window of the dining hall aboard the HMS Erasmus. I took a stroll on deck and felt a twinge of pain in my hip, nothing a nip of the whiskey in my quarters wouldn't fix I told myself. The only thing a nip of whiskey can't fix is, of course, running out of whiskey!

I found the elevator towards the bridge observation lounge and spied the captain and crew hard at work. Lord Disraeli and Jennings stood next to the captain inspecting a voluminous manifest of some kind. I took great pains for them not to see me, as I wanted them both occupied while testing the limits of the master skeleton key Jennings had given me.

I had noticed on my stroll a small door leading to the cargo hold on deck. I made my way there without encountering a soul and quietly slipped the master key from my breast pocket into the lock. It made a satisfying click as the door swung open. I made my way down a steep flight of iron stairs in the gloom but was limited in my capacity for descent by my accursed hip. A single spot light illuminated the hold, filled with all manner of crates and carriage for the voyage. My eyes adjusted to the light, and soon I saw sitting on the floor of the three-deck-high hold the same metal levithan Yuan Tsu and I had spied through the woods on the low road, its four wheels and bible black body cleansed of mud. Two men with mops drenched from nearby saltwater buckets stood cleaning the inside of the vehicle's main compartment, which had been shut three days previously. The metal lined compartment was huge with enough room for two of Barnum's Circus elephants.

I turned to climb the stairs back to the door when the key fell from my grasp and fell silently on a pile of towels three decks below. Hidden from view by the bulkhead, I waited until the men finished their work and left, then climbed down the stairs in absolute agony. As I retrieved the key I heard a sound of someone snoring through a cast iron door to my right. The snoring echoed cavernously in the hold, as deep in tone as the church pipe organ back home in Stormview. I decided to push my luck, and my hip, to the limit, and once again found the master key to be worth its moniker as I unlocked the door. Inside the room was an iron cage so large it stretched from the floor nearly two decks up. Straw lined and empty save a bucket holding water, there lay sleeping in the center a creature of such remarkable proportions that I nearly yelled in amazement. I knew instantly that this must be the great beast whose cry awakened me three nights earlier. I heard voices in the hold outside and quickly darted behind a stack of crates full of corn beef hash. Three men entered dressed in the same attire as the men in the woods, one of them with a fresh cast on his left arm.

"What are you supposed to do?" said one of the men.

"Shoot him full of lots more drugs." said the other man, loading one of the strange glass chambered rifles with darts, one by one.

"He looks pretty drugged to me already." said the man with the cast on his arm.

"Disraeli says take no chances." The man with the rifle said, firing six darts into the sleeping creature.

"My arm is killing me." said the man with the cast.

"You're lucky he didn't pull it right out of your socket and beat you like a drum," said the other man, laughing.

"Bunyip would have." said the man with the rifle.

"Bunyip would have started with your head." a shuddering sound came from the three men as they left the room, pulling the door behind them.

I took a last gander at the mighty beast, such a kind face he had somehow. I went to exit the door and found no latch on the inside. I was trapped like the great creature before me, and my lunch with Disraeli was certainly beginning and my absence duly noted. I sat down on the jailer's stool in the corner by a pile of straw and lit up my pipe.

The smoke wafted out into the room, animated by the one electric light above the latchless door. Kentucky Dark-Fired, robust and good for clearing the mind, which at that moment I sorely needed. The smoke reached the nose of the creature and suddenly he began to stir.

"Where am I?" the creature spoke through a haze of my smoke. "You are the man from Yuan Tsu's cabin."

"Yes I am' I said, the very moorings of what I believed to be true in this world coming apart at the seams.

"What is your name?" he said.

"I'm Sam Clemons to my friends, Mark Twain to my readers, some of whom are friends hopefully." I rambled, not sure what exactly to tell this strange beast.

"And what is your name?" I asked.

"Skookum, Sasquatch to the canoe riders, your kind calls me the Wood Ghost, my mother named me little foot on the day she died". The creature wiggled his toes, nearly three feet in length.

"More like a Bigfoot I'd say." I said. The creature raised its head with a look of puzzlement.

"Why are you here Mark Twain?" he asked. "May I call you that? I am not one of your readers."

"You can, you speak quite well, any fool can learn to read." I said, relighting my pipe.

"Would you teach me?" Bigfoot said "And may I have some of your tobacco?"

"Yes, and yes." In a display of bravado and human kindness I'm not especially known for, I offered the beast my freshly packed pipe through the narrow iron bars, risking summary dislocation of my arms and possible decapitation. As I reached in with a hearty flame from my chrome and ivory lighter, he took such a draw off the pipe as to render the tobacco in the bowl a mote of dust in mere seconds.

"Thank you Mark Twain, you may call me Bigfoot, I like this name." he said, slumping back against the wall and passing out. The red feathered vanes of at least twenty spent darts clung to his fur.

"Looks like we are both prisoners here my friend, sleep well." I sat back down on the stool and wondered how long it would take before I was discovered here. Maritime justice can be quite harsh, although I discounted being slapped in irons for merely being curious.

Suddenly the door opened. In stepped Lord Disraeli and Jennings. Jennings carried a silver serving tray laden with sandwiches and cakes. Lord Disraeli produced a flask of whiskey and took a healthy swig, his fox-like gaze fixating on me in the dim light.

"Lunch?" he said.

LUNCH WITH
A WHISKEY-TONGUED
YANKEE DEVIL

November 15th, 1893

Dear Desdimona,

I t is possible today that I, Lord Benjamin Disraeli, Ben to my friends of which I have none, have met his match in words in a mister Mark Twain. Like many Americans this is not a real name but a pseudonym given to themselves and laden with personal meaning. In England one must be born to greatness and opportunity, here in the new world one merely claims the horizon towards which one walks as their own.

I am here bobbing aboard the Erasmus in the pacific near Hawaii, the good ol girl showing her metal tenfold in speed and comfort. Mr Twain arrived late and was given the quarters you suggested. He simply could not resist a good riddle, and immediately used the master key to gain access to the hold. Mr Twain wound up trapped in one of my cells holding the creature known as Sasquatch. He is the fourteenth specimen of his kind to make the sea voyage to the arena in Melbourne, and none too soon! Indeed I feared not being able to procure another Sasquatch until a chinese local to Seattle showed us the way. The actual capture was a dreadful, highly inefficient affair. The men are tired, many of them dead so, along with nearly all the dogs.

There are many land disputes in the near east that need to be resolved involving Victoria and her dear cousin the Czar, and only a successful blood match between the two powers will settle anything. The Russias have chosen the large wombat and salt water crocs for their champions, since they lack any indigenous cryptids. Several other matches on the Christmas ticket are shaping up as well! A frankly quite annoying birdlike creature found in a crypt near Cairo is being pitted against another lot from the Caucasus demanding access to the Suez. He is called the Kren and will most likely fight the giant scorpions we captured in Baja. The new Yeti only fights if we hold a rifle to the head of his baby daughter, but fights quite well under those pressures it seems. And of course Bunyip. He still slaughters all challengers, and there are many challengers these days as you know. The only creature Bunyip hasn't faced is the Kraken, and with his experience as a water dweller I don't think the tentacled beast would last long against his ruthless cunning. Bunyip still patrols the Melbourne sewers for our other syndicates, and doesn't seem to care much who he is asked to kill. The electric cattle prods that finally got him out of the swamps apparently have had a lasting impact on his loyalties. He seems lost, killing without pleasure, which is worrisome. I still think he is planning something, but I'm not certain of what.

And finally this Mark Twain, the father of what passes for literature there in our former colonies. Suffice to say he is now aware of our attempts to recruit him to the cause of global gladiatorial politics, where creatures whose very existence is hotly debated fight to the death to settle all manner of disputes. We are well paid for the procurement and exhibitionary fees for such contests, with a limitless horizon for our profits. I thought the partitioning of the Dardanelles a particularly righteous victory for our cause through skillful cryptid pugilism, without a single human life lost, and Johnny Turk sent back to Asia Minor at last.

Twain's fame and reputation for modernistic thinking, speaking to the aspiration and limitless ambitions of the new world, would go a long way in attracting the lesser nations of the globe. They are distrustful for good reason of us, the old guard, the old gold. It gleams still, my sweet. I just can't tell yet if Twain, like Bunyip, isn't hiding some other motive. His lecture in Melbourne will no doubt be well attended, and the Christmas fight ticket in the arena is the same night. We shall know then if he is indeed our man in America.

With much affection,
Your adoring cousin,
Disraeli

LUNCH WITH THE PREENING
LORD OF
OUR FORMER MASTERS

Without a word as to my predicament being locked in a restricted area on board a ship under his charter, Lord Disraeli served me tea and sandwiches for an hour at midday. I simply puffed my pipe and listened to the sound of Bigfoot snoring in the cage next to me until finally he did indeed speak.

"I could have you hanged sir, for trespassing in a restricted area of her majesty's ship the Erasmus." Disraeli quipped between bites of provolone and watercress. The extreme nature of his stick made me curious as to the nature of the forthcoming carrot.

"Really?" I laughed. " A good old fashioned hanging by the mizzen mast? Or will I be hung from these new fancy and aromatic steam engines of yours?

Disraeli stopped for a moment. "You are clever Mr. Twain, surely clever enough to realize your predicament."

"With respect, I see no such predicament for me, Mr. Disraeli.. There are no postings as to this area's restrictions in any language known to me. The master key was provided to me upon boarding with no explicit areas of non-access described or reasonably implied. I am a guest aboard your vessel bearing associations of two friendly governments, one a colony in your government's empire, one a former colony and my country of citizenship. A country with considerable interests and firepower within your empire's sphere of influence. I can only infer that failing to buy my support for whatever purpose this noble creature serves for you, you intend to blackmail me for a simple act of curiosity and dare I say, empathy for another living soul."

Disraeli slammed his fork down. "This soul of yours killed fifteen of my men, including my cousin Desdimona's youngest nephew."

"Was he expected to simply walk into that cage of yours willingly, after being attacked by hounds, after being shot with god knows what in your darts?" I said.

"Darts is it?" said Disraeli, regaining his composure. "I love to play. My offices in parliament had a board and were open to all challengers from either side of the aisle." Disraeli stood as Jennings began clearing the food away.

"I'm a billiards man, the geometry is a comfort to me. The devil take darts, along with your incomprehensible game of cricket." I said, baiting him. His face boiled red as he turned to leave.

"Dinner tonight Mr. Twain, Samuel, at my table, with the captain? He is a big fan of your Tom Sawyer. There are a few things about our business in Melbourne that I would like to explain to you. said Disaeli

"This hip is all the pain I need Lord Disraeli, but I do appreciate any opportunity to engage in conversation, may I go now?" I said, rising from the jailer's stool.

"Yes, of course, there is another elevator beyond the staircase in the hold, Jennings will show you the way." Disraeli said, defeated.

"I'll find my way, see you at dinner." I said.

Suddenly, the Master's Mate burst into the room, his face flushed with excitment. "Lord Disraeli, a whale has been sighted tailing the ship!

"Excellent!" shouted Disraeli "A fresh shot at some fresh meat, uncover the steam harpoon!"

THE CALL OF YUAN TSU

Twain boarded the Erasmus, as agreed, and he handed me the payment for his month at large in a leather valise plus a bonus of fifty dollars for safe delivery from our ordeal in the woods. I did not accept this bonus verbally when he offered it, but found it in the final payment anyway, concealed in a compartment with a card reading "Never refuse gifts from a man rightly delivered from peril! Yours in the brotherhood of survival, Mark Twain"

As Twain ambled away towards the docks my worry quickly shifted to my lead Pony, whom I'd owned for three years now. The journey back at such a clip had rendered her lame, so I loaded a round into my colt and released her from her earthly labor. This obligation was carried out in front of Hadden's Butchery and Livery Mercantile, Pike Street Market, Seattle. Hadden himself began the butchering and paid me an extra five dollars for the sad remnants of this loyal mount.

I took my earnings to a local tavern and soon a full measure of whiskey was mine, a well deserved tonic for the span of stress, danger, and risks absorbed of late from these lands. I sat there at the bar considering selling the cabin, wagon, and last of my horses and returning to Shanghai, when I heard the unmistakable sounds of a soul slapped in irons. The soul belonged to a friend, the Beast Sasquatch, with whom I'd acquainted myself ten years earlier.

After saving my life at the hands of a drunken band of Suquamish braves, Sasquatch had nursed me back to health in his cave dwelling hidden deep in the eastern woods. There were moments after my rescue where I assumed indeed I had died. Laden with fever, the visage of a twelve foot high monkey man spooning mushroom and pine nut broth into my broken windpipe was a challenge to what my eyes had considered normal up until then. And my ears for that matter, for after several weeks the beast spoke to me in clipped pigeon Cantonese. He had been raised by a French Fur trapper and his Shoshone wife, part of the Lewis and Clark Corp of Discovery that had opened these lands to the broader world. These events were well known and had occurred some eighty years previously, and I took the unlikely life-spanned truth of this in stride given the extraordinary fact of his mere existence.

We became friends, and when my legs healed enough I limped with him down to the beach some three miles inland. Standing together on a high seaside cliff with a clear trespass to the water below, the beast called out over the water with a mighty "Yip Yip". The phrase reminded me of the tonal enunciations of the Canary Island dwellers who communicated over vast, echoing distances. Soon to my great surprise, a great gray whale spout trumpeted out a mere two hundred yards off shore. Sasquatch leapt from the cliff and disappeared into the boiling surf below, only to reemerge riding on the back of the great whale. As they surfaced, Sasquatch hurled salmon four feet in length by the tail, spinning wildly until landing with a thump against the treeline behind me. He repeated this ballet with the whale and the waves four or five times. The impact of the silver salmon upon the pines rendered them decidedly deceased and ready for a feast that night, which after weeks of the pine nut gruel restored me to reasonable health. We returned to the cliff several times over the next few weeks with the beast teaching me the method of calling the great whale, an art he'd practiced his whole life.

Some time the next week I returned to Seattle and had the good fortune of joining a poker game along with an eastern fellow unfamiliar with the west coast hold 'em' favored in the gambling halls along Pike Street. After some losses I pried from him on an inside straight the deed to his cabin, buckboard, and two mules whom I eventually replaced with two paints. To what end the mules came I do not know.

This is how I came to know Mark Twain ten years later, whose request for a secluded place to write came down to me through Earl Liscombe, chancellor of the Seattle Literacy Society and a drinking companion of mine. On the eve of the solicitation he had with him a British fellow by the name of Jennings. After several rounds of Whiskey (paid for by this Jennings), I made the mistake of revealing the existence, but not location, of the beast Sasquatch. This divulgement set into motion the series of events which led to Sasquatch's capture at the hands of the strange men and machine in the woods. So deep was my shame knowing I had compromised my friend that I withheld the truth from Twain as we fled from the scene of the apprehension, and prayed that somehow Sasquatch had prevailed.

Indeed, he had prevailed, by that meaning he still lived and breathed, albeit in heavy chains.

Inside the tavern, nursing a large Whiskey and contemplating my return home to China, I heard above a mechanical thrum the beast's unmistakable bass-baritone coming from some muffled source outside. Thirty feet from the front door I could see the great machine from the woods making its way towards the docks. Its four great wheels turned upon the cobble stones, followed by at least twenty of the men with their strange rifles. A narrow sluice in the main compartment some three feet across was the source of the mournful wailing sound I'd heard at the bar. As the beast moaned, one of the men fired another dart into the sluice, and the poor creature's cries ceased.

I followed the men and machine to the docks where a giant crane stood poised above the waiting hold of the Erasmus. Soon the crane had gripped the black iron compartment and lifted the whole machine into the gaping maw and a great iron door shut with a colossal K-rang!

Where the men were taking this noble soul I did not know. I knew the fault of his capture lay with me, and honor dictated in that moment that I act. I ran to the end of the half mile jetty extending into the bay from the docks, and quickly repeated the "Yip Yip" Sasquatch had made to his friend the whale ten years earlier.

How I had remembered the call after so long I do not know, but memory obliged me and soon the words echoed out across the water. I repeated the query several times to no avail, then heard the sounds of the mooring horn from the HMS Erasmus. Soon, they would be disembarking, and my friend's fate would be sealed in a manner of his captor's choosing.

Returning to the dock I spied the man Jennings, the Britisher and associate of my friend Earl Lipscomb, posted at the gangplank, conferring with another white man with curly black hair. At that moment I knew Jennings had been the one who had somehow discovered the beast's whereabouts in the woods, and likely directed the men with rifles to his capture. I knew as well the likelihood of my own death should I reveal myself and confront him with such an accusation, given my status as a chinaman in this place, and the obvious power he wielded. Instead, I undertook a bold plan. Returning to Hadden's Livery and Mercantile, I sold him my wagon and remaining horse. I then walked to the local assay office above Pike Street and drew up a bill of sale for the cabin and seventeen acres surrounding.

They gave me a most fair price for the property due no doubt to the possibility of gold in the nearby creek.

After a quick trip to my cousin's boarding house on telegraph street and nearly three hours following Sasquatch cries of enslavement upon my ears, I returned to dock where the HMS Erasmus had just sounded three bells indicating her imminent disembarkation. I then took a path that many Chinese had done in the past to obtain entry into nations exclusionary to our kind, and knocked upon the servant's entrance aft of the vessel, and waited for the porter. He answered, also Chinese, and without a word I handed him an envelope filled with seven hundred United States Notes. He pointed to the stairs heading below deck to the servants quarters where I would plan the next phase of Sasquatch's rescue. I knew it would involve me calling for help upon the open ocean, the great whale he would sometimes ride, in order to save us and bring us back safely to land.

OF HARPOONS AND DISRAELI

It seemed the whole crew had crowded up on deck to watch the great steam harpoon's deployment. As I loaded a much needed plug of tobacco into my pipe, sea birds of all kinds flapped overhead in the prussian blue perfection of an early morning breeze. Land was now four days behind the HMS Erasmus, two of which I had spent imprisoned below deck on my ill-advised mission of investigation into the beast Bigfoot. The fate to befall him at the hands of these men I now knew, and I feared for him and his Cryptid brethren in the Melbourne arena, 80 days' journey from now.

At least I was a free man again. Disraeli seemed to forget himself entirely after our battle of wits (which no doubt my Yankee probity had won) in favor of a most unusual contest; a great blue whale now following the Erasmus in perfect cadence. It was his intent to kill the beast and procure the ambergris within its cranium while at sea, discarding the carcass for the birds above and sharks below.

Disraeli lept to the iron platform that held the harpoon, a sixteen foot marvel of engineering hitherto not seen upon the waters. With such firepower I feared Whales of all oceans would follow in the path of the American Buffalo and Passenger Pigeon, decimated beyond the hope of recovery by man's industrial hunger for the fruits of their valuable flesh.

Jennings did his best to limit Disraeli's enthusiasm for the endeavor, employing him to not miss the target with a premature shot. Six such shots were possible, each harpoon with a six-prong spike held in a neat row upon the firing wall.

"Good man Jennings" said Disraeli, eyeing the target through the telescope gun-sight of the harpoon. "I will do my best not to shoot too high and wound the surrounding ocean."

The great whale trumpeted as it snaked in between the great steam fired wake of the Erasmus. From the hold below I could hear the sound of Bigfoot, screaming in anguish and pounding upon his iron cage. Immediately the unmistakable sounds of tranquilizer rifle fire silenced the great beast, and Disraeli continued on.

Disraeli fired once and missed to the port side of the whale, nearly as long as three London street cars. The power of the harpoon's lance as it rocketed from the barrel under steam power was truly sobering.. I was sickened by the whole affair as another bolt was loaded.

"It seems rather like the animal is chasing us to some end, wouldn't you say Mr. Twain?" said Disraeli.

"Of that I have no idea sir, I only know you are a coward as well as a brigand, and I take leave of your hospitality." by this meaning the palace-like comfort of my quarters, in favor of the modest room provided me by the Melbourne Literary Society. I should very well miss the whiskey and hot bath dispensary.

Another shot fired, another miss.

"Blast" said Disraeli "Jennings, what in blazes am I doing wrong?"

"Try adjusting the gunsight 10 degrees aft sir, to calculate for the cross wind, then you should have him sir." said Jennings, shoveling another lance into the barrel of the great weapon.

Disraeli adjusted the sight and was preparing to dispense death and judgment to the leviathan tailing them, when lo and behold Yuan Tsu appeared out of nowhere, brandishing his colt revolver, aimed squarely between Disraeli's eyes. Quickly Disraeli's men along with the quartermaster of the Erasmus drew their sidearms and drew a bead on Yuan Tsu who cocked the hammer of the revolver.

"Hold your fire!" yelled Jennings, his own hand gripping the pistol in his belt.

"Who in blazes is this Chinese? Who are you sir?" said Disraeli, alarmed and perturbed at the interruption of his contest with the whale.

"My name is Yuan Tsu, I am known to your associate Mr Jennings, who knows me to be a man willing to pull this trigger." said Yuan Tsu, delicately balancing the outcome of his own predicament.

"Jennings?" said Disraeli.

"This man is known to me. Yes, it was from him we learned of the beast below in irons, and by following his and Mr. Twain's movements into the woods.

I looked at Yuan Tsu in disbelief, not able to comprehend his role in such a tragedy.

"Release the animal held below now, cast him into the ocean, and do unto me as you will. Otherwise your brains will be the next thing swabbed from this deck" said Yuan Tsu.

"Sir, lookout!" yelled the midshipmen.

In an instant the knife's edge standoff between the men gave way to sheer pandemonium as the HMS Erasmus was rocked sideways by the great blue whale whom mere moments previously had been skirting her wake. Yuan Tsu lost his footing and tumbled over the deck into the cold water below. His colt revolver slid across the deck and landed at my feet. I reached down and grabbed it, placing it in the folds of my jacket as the men began firing into the froth below at Yuan Tsu.

I, BUNYIP

First, I bit off the leader's head, flashing my teeth in an intimidating style I called 'teethy teeth teeth'. This flourish no doubt motivated his lackey and partner in crime to confess the location of the gold stolen from the Adelaide Mining Company. I had him indicate the hiding place on a map I carried for such confessions and extolled him to be accurate in his recollections. He appeared to be certain that the gold was in a cistern fourteen miles outside Melbourne near the northern railroad line. I complimented him on his honesty and also the excellent hiding place. Then I killed him too by slitting his throat with my left foreclaw. My right foreclaw still needed some time to recover following my previous match in the Melbourne Arena against all manner of giant Crocs, Dingo, and Roos. I was their champion. I fought for myself, and for the thrill of being free to kill within the world of men.

It was getting late, and my work for the night was more butchery for Disraeli. Fourteen years had passed since he had hired Ransom Pike Sullivan to flush me from the Adelaide swamps and bring me here to Melbourne, the arena, and the mean streets where I did his bidding.

Not that I minded, death had been my business in one way or another since before dreamtime started, before the aborigines as the whites called them arrived over the landbridge near Darwin. My kind were once plentiful and formidable, somewhere between predator and scavenger, until the arrival of man when all became their prey. Let me tell you a story, and how my fate became intertwined with the creature Bigfoot, and the man Mark Twain.

Tun, that was my name, when my family was still alive. We had come across the great land bridge together between Indonesia and Australia, whose great span now lays covered by sea. Upon arriving there was no such thing as a man, only us, and when men arrived they began killing us and gave us the collective name of 'Bunyip'. We, and justly so in my opinion, began killing them back.

But first we had this flat place all to ourselves for what seemed an eternity, and my kind knows the meaning of eternity as much as a living creature can, save the trees who live longest of all. It was after half of this eternity spent hunting and living beneath the stars that things began to change, for the worse too. A great fire exploded in the sky one night, bringing daylight, then a great darkness after which the sun did not appear for a long, long time.

During this period we slept in the manner of our kind, below ground in the wet earth, eyes closed, not stirring season after season, one of us waking to burrow upwards and see if the food had returned. When we finally awoke most of the creatures we hunted no longer roamed, and my father and mother did not wake with us. We changed and adapted along with other creatures until the great fire was forgotten even by us Bunyips, although we were not yet called that. Much, much later, the very first men arrived over the landbridge, and when the bridge sank beneath the waves the men stayed and never left. We hid.

A billabong is a foul place to hide, but hide we did for millennia untold after the first men started hunting us. Then after a length of time quite long for men, the white men arrived in their ships upon the water. They killed the other men there long before them, and killed us with even more ruthless abandon with far more powerful weapons. We Bunyips, of which I am the last known, have several weapons that kept both black and white men at bay until at last succumbing to the inevitable. We did not go down without a fight, and the fear of those fights endure in the stories they tell their children, who are quite tasty indeed.

My favorite weapon for hunting a man is his own fear. One sight of my quilted fangs and dagger-like claws snuffs out any flame of fight in them, most of them at least. Most run, others beg for mercy I would never give them, and the last thing they hear as I slash their throat is my voice speaking to them in their native tongue. I know several of the tongues of man, and my power of mimicry lures them into the soft quicksand surrounding the billabong where they become frozen in their steps, their clunky boots, and soon I'm whispering their names in a final mockery.

You could certainly say this cruel, horribly so. But, if you knew of the cruelty in which they wiped out every single member of my family you might find your way to sympathy, or at least an understanding. For the last thing *they* heard were the words of men laughing as they killed them with spears, the fire-hardened edge of a boomerang, or much later the pitiless barrel of a white man's rifle. Had it not been for these white men and their sophisticated weapons I would still be hidden deep in a billabong, waiting until my next victim happened along. They always happened along.

Most of the time I hid, not making a sound as they gathered above me with their whale-oil lamps and dogs. The dogs could follow my scent well enough, but the stench of the billabongs stopped them from knowing exactly where I was hidden. Often the men would fire round after round into the black slime hoping one would find its mark on me, but they never came close and soon I slipped away undetected into the night. One such night though, things changed. Ransom Pike Sullivan changed them, and me, forever.

Two nights earlier outside of Adelaide I had become hungry. I usually hunt/eat once per month beneath the sickle moon when the white men hunt for wombats at night for their rich and lustrous fur. When they hunt in pairs my job is much easier as I usually kill one of them then use his choked pleas for mercy to lure his partner into the shadows where I wait. Sometimes I force the first man to slow down and beg for his life in a calm tone, so as to more easily mimic his voice later. "Slow down, tell me your name." Things like that. I am good at my job.

So on such a sickle moon night I heard the sound of men above my slimy billabong, smacking the bush with heavy canes as was the usual Wombat technique. I surfaced slowly, the near moonless night affording the perfect hunting conditions. But something was wrong. The night smelled of a lightning storm, dry and far away, the burnt air filling my nostrils. Making the biggest mistake of my life I crept from the billabong and raised up.

I heard a man yell "Now!" and I was suddenly enveloped in a white hot blinding light as bright as daylight. I shielded my eyes, the incandescent curtain blinding me through my six digit claws. I heard a soft popping sound, like the sound of a man's arm separating from its socket, and a burning sensation in my side. My sight became fuzzy as three more pops hissed from the direction of the light, each followed by a thorn's prick on my body. Panicked, I dove for the safety of the billabong, deep to twenty times a man's height just next to me, my sanctuary, in an instant I would be free.

My body thrashed as I fell into a large net the men had somehow placed on the surface of the billabong. I had been netted before so I began slashing at an angle against the net, to no avail. Unlike the hemp nets I'd cut with ease, this net was some type of fine metal, which I then began to pull apart. Just as the net began to give way I heard the same voice give another command. "Juice!" he called, and the net pulsed with some unseen force. My body stiffened like a kangaroo struck by lightning as the world around me turned to fire. Then, there was nothing. Until I awoke in the arena. I remained in the Melbourne Arena where I fought battle after battle at the behest of Lord Disraeli until meeting the creature Bigfoot, and his friend Mark Twain, some fifteen years later. Up until then I had been happy in my work, or at least thought as much.

IN THE MATTER OF
RANSOM PIKE SULLIVAN

Sullivan is the name. Born County Clare, Ireland, 1830, no good to anyone but no worse for wear. Tracker mostly, of men and beast, mostly stolen cattle, I came to

New South Wales by way of Darwin in the year 1845 to escape the great famine that began that year. Everyone I'd loved had died and lay black in the ground along with the gray slime of the spuds near the town of Ennis. To pay for my passage I placed myself in the service of one Benjamin Disraeli, through one his agents in Galway. At the docks in Dublin there were two ships, one bound for America, and one for the new world. I wanted to see America, and nearly absconded with Disraeli's wages but knew better than to cross a man of such power and titles. I boarded a coal ship bound for Melbourne and never returned to Ireland again. Disraeli later told me that as wise a decision it was of mine not to cross him, it was an equally foolish one to come to be in his employ, laughing as he said it.

Upon arrival in New South Wales I began tracking men for the right honorable Lord Disraeli and his Australian holding company, mostly men fleeing with stolen gold, silver, gems, and other such things that desperate men confuse with real value. Real value is measured in freedom, not much freedom in being hung by the neck or locked away if you ask me, although some would say in death there comes the ultimate freedom. Not really sure.

Lord Disraeli gave me wide latitude in the manner I went about my tracking, on account of him eventually becoming the Prime Minister of Great Britain and never setting foot down under. In fact we never met face to face until he began to build the Arena in 1882 outside of Melbourne. Of course by then he was also stone dead, but that is a tale for another time.

The Arena was a kind of race track, and the race upon that track was a race to the death. Instead of wagering on the ponies in pounds sterling, men of great power and influence placed bets with deeds to land and sea, great canals, railways, in proxy to their King or Queen, dividing up the globe into assets to be won or lost. The outcomes of these battles were decided by beasts of a most curious nature fighting for their very lives in gladiatorial combat. When I say curious beasts I mean exactly that, for the tales told as children had a strange way of becoming true when it came to Lord Disraeli and the Arena.

Lord Disraeli had at his disposal great resources, and in 1882 he gave me full control of these resources in order to stock his Arena with champions. We combed the old world for beasts of legend including the Yeti of Nepal, the Kren of Egypt, the Mande Burung of India, The Moa of New Zealand, all manner of Tigers, Crocodiles, and leviathan from the depths of the oceans. These, such as the Kraken, were kept in great Salt Water tanks and used in combat sparingly to great effect. The Suez Canal changed hands twice during battles with the Kraken and a squadron of vicious Octopi. Ten years passed with grand spectacles sparing the world of its young men going to die for the rights to a region or territory both sides claimed.

But, over time, people became bored, and Lord Disraeli had to find new, exciting champions for his Arena, still in its red Spanish brick prime as a venue. He did this in part for the greater good of mankind, however, his personal profit from such exhibitions was directly tied to the manner in which he unnaturally sustained his life, but again, I digress.

In early 1893 a wire came from London that a new beast from the west coast of America near Washington Territory had been found. The beasts were ape-like, and since we had exhausted our supply of Ape Giganticus from Indochina, replacements of a simian nature were needed and needed badly. Something about something that looks like a man fighting for its life makes people part with their folding money shall we say.

From what Mr. Jennings, Lord Disraeli's man, said in his cable, the capture was going to be as difficult as the Yeti, perhaps more so. So, we loaded up the full contingent of men, hounds, tranq rifles, and the new ironclad steam driven land cart, and set forth for America aboard the HMS Erasmus, itself a new and glittering modern technological marvel. Before leaving Melbourne I had some quick words for Bunyip, who was working the sewers for Lord Disraeli, keeping the local syndicates in line.

I had brought Bunyip to the Arena twenty years earlier, and he had gradually become part of Lord Disraeli's operation. He still fought in the arena, but also worked outside of it at night, returning to his iron cage before dawn. I think it was mostly because he knew there was nowhere to hide in Australia once I arrived, and that if he escaped it would mean a death sentence. I neither trusted nor liked the beast, and its power of mimicry unnerved everyone, even Lord Disraeli. But never more a savage killer of men and beast there was. Our conversation that night before leaving for America was typical of our dealings.

"Lord Disraeli says you're killing too many Indonesians. Ease up, they've begun to cooperate and we don't want to overplay our hand." I said.

"Of course." he said, his head sticking out of a sewer grate near the main rail line.

"It will be several months before I return, just stick to the plan, win your fights, and we'll keep you in your own cell as we always have," I said, flicking a match down onto the wet street after lighting my cigarette.

"Yes, I see. Where are you going? What champion will you be returning with?" Bunyip said, strangely interested.

"America." I said.

"How nice." He said in a more or less cordial manner. "Why do you ask?" I said curiously.

"Just bored I guess, like your guests in the arena, something is lacking there after so many years of predictable bloodshed." said Bunyip, sharpening his claw on the metal grate.

"Well, from what I hear, this champion will bring a little excitement back to the game. Just do as Lord Disraeli asks and I'll see you around the annual Christmas Eve Match." I said, throwing down the cigarette and rubbing it out with my foot.

"Why do you always light a cigarette and then extinguish it after one puff?" the beast asked.

"Too many of these things will kill you." I said. "They killed Lord Disraeli."

"Yes, but he still walks, talks, and takes his measure of this world wouldn't you say?" said Bunyip.

"Yes, indeed he does, and it is strange his still bein' here, but then again I'm sittin' here talking to a giant killing machine with seven inch fangs at no o'clock in the morning. Good lord preserve ya, ya beastie." I said, walking down the alley towards the main street in the pitch black night.

"Indeed." I heard the Bunyip say, slithering back into the sewer and closing the grate after him.

Two days after we put to sea, Bunyip went on a killing spree so savage that his liberty about town was completely restricted, and Lord Disreai nearly had him finished off. What spared his life? The new champion, the creature Bigfoot, who would need a worthy adversary in the arena upon his arrival.

YUAN TSU TOODLE-LOO

The calamity on deck caused me to drop my smoking pipe, a first for me in all my years of serious knickerbockering. Through the gold fields and dusty horse towns of the Sierra's, through brawls in San Francisco taverns on Market Street, never once had I dropped my pipe. But thus I did and thus it shattered into a million porcelain fragments upon the ground. I really miss that pipe. And my friend Yuan Tsu, who made an unexpected appearance aboard deck brandishing his colt revolver in defense of the great grey whale following the HMS Erasmus, and this the incident that caused my fingers to slip and render me potentially pipeless for the rest of the journey, a fate worse than colic to a smoking man.

Being a civilized vessel the captain eventually allowed me to win by means of poker, a spare left by a passenger on the maiden voyage of the Erasmus from Portsmouth to Melbourne that spring. He was intent upon the rescue of our friend in irons below, Bigfoot, I came to find out later through reasoning mostly inductive, and also by a great deal of conjecture, as I never spoke to Yuan Tsu again, his fate lost beneath the waves of the Pacific.

From what I could gather, Yuan Tsu had stealthily boarded the Erasmus via the servant's quarters upon our embarkation, paying the ship's quartermaster to hold his tongue inking the final crew manifest. On the day of his regrettable loss, Yuan Tsu sat below deck near the hold as Disraeli made every attempt to win me to his cause at the Melbourne Arena. In exchange for my wholehearted endorsement of his venture I would receive something few artists ever receive in their lifetimes, a seat at the table of power, something I had never wished for and still don't. If I could change the world I most certainly would not meddle on such a grand scale the fates and fashions of human beings, leaving that to our lord and savior, whomever you believe that to be.

As we made our way to the deck to witness Lord Disraeli's attempt at harpooning the curious pursuing whale, Yuan Tsu quickly snuck in behind us in an attempt to free our friendly beast in chains. And to what end this prison break upon the open ocean I will now explain. Bigfoot was a whale rider, apparently from birth, and the whale in pursuit of us was his lifelong friend. Bigfoot had indeed called the animal, explaining the curious "Yip

Yip" I had heard each night before retiring to my smoking chamber.

When Bigfoot heard the steam harpoon's lances being propelled at his friend the whale, he quickly had Yuan Tsu unlock the cage and bade him try and stop the intended carnage above. The reason for this request was the great iron chain around Bigfoot's ankle, for with no key in sight the brute had but brute force to free himself first before any help could be offered. Yuan Tsu ran for the ladder up out of the hold and up to the deck where his pistol was indeed brandished and his request most duly made to Disraeli. Then, calamity struck.

Two armed men woke from their lay-about ways below deck and discovered the creature Bigfoot nearly free of his bondage. They quickly discharged their tranquilizer rifle darts into the beast, rendering him unconscious once again. On deck, the situation was made infinitely worse by the great grey whale exacting his revenge upon the keel of the Erasmus, sending her lurching portside and dislodging several of the lifeboats.

Yuan Tsu lost his footing and fell over into the boiling surf, never to be seen again. Disraeli would have certainly seen to it that his days remain numbered should he return to any civilized quarter of the world.

The whale disappeared as quickly as it had come, and soon the Erasmus was back on track to New South Wales, Melbourne, and Bigfoot's now unavoidable fate in the arena. I decided to play my affection for the talking beast down, and infer to Disraeli that maybe, just maybe, I might be persuaded to see his point of view. This was not my intent dear reader, as you will soon see in the next volume of this work. But first, you must find where I have hidden it!

END BOOK ONE